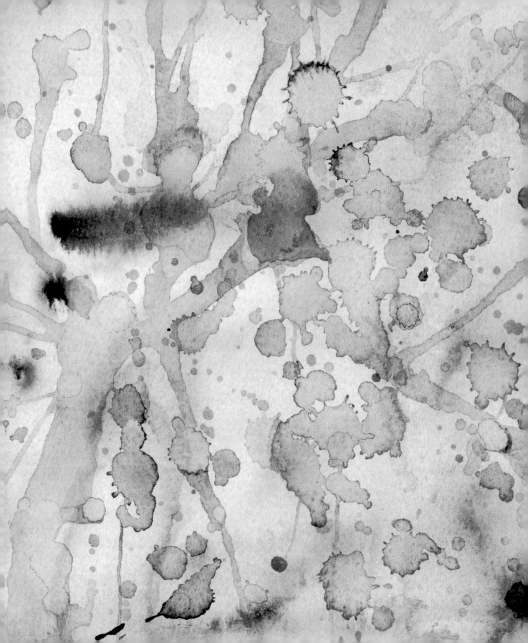

For Sue

First published 1994 by Walker Books Ltd
87 Vauxhall Walk, London SE11 5HJ

This edition published 2009

2 4 6 8 10 9 7 5 3 1

This book has been typeset in AT Arta

Printed in China

British Library Cataloguing in Publication Data:
a catalogue record for this book is available from the British Library.

ISBN 978-0-7445-3518-1

www.walker.co.uk

Caveman Dave

Nick Sharratt

WALKER BOOKS
AND SUBSIDIARIES
LONDON · BOSTON · SYDNEY · AUCKLAND

Caveman Dave
lives in a cave.

He's smelly but
he's very brave.

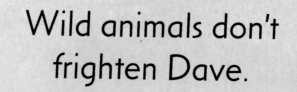

Wild animals don't frighten Dave.

At bears and tigers
he will wave.

He tells fierce mammoths
to behave.

Dave really is
extremely brave –

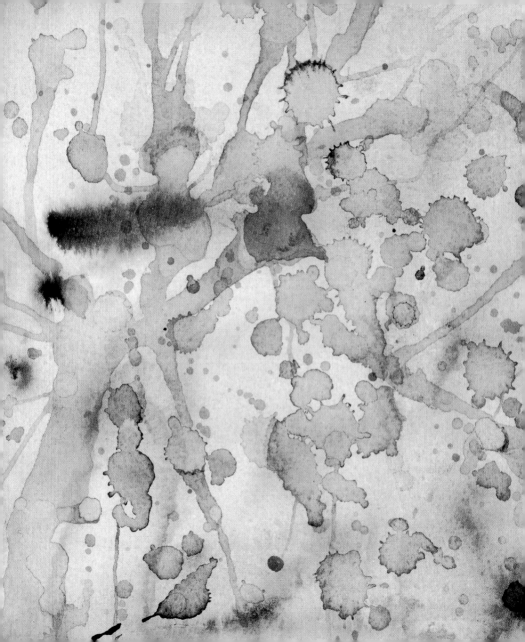

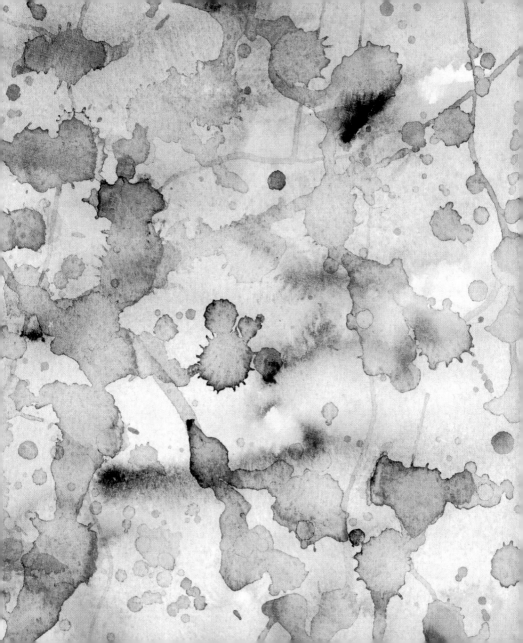